A NOTE TO PARENTS

Early Step into Reading Books are designed for preschoolers and kindergartners who are just getting ready to read. The words are easy, the type is big, and the stories are packed with rhyme, rhythm, and repetition.

We suggest that you read this book to your child the first few times, pointing to each word as you go. Soon your child will start saying the words with you. And before long, he or she will try to read the story alone. Don't be surprised if your child uses the pictures to figure out the text— that's what they're there for! The important thing is to develop your child's confidence—and to show your child that reading is fun.

When your child is ready to move on, try the rest of the steps in our Step into Reading series. **Step 1 Books** (preschool–grade 1) feature the same easy-to-read type as the Early Step into Reading Books, but with more words per page. **Step 2 Books** (grades 1–3) are both longer and slightly more difficult, while **Step 3 Books** (grades 2–3) introduce readers to paragraphs and fully developed plot lines. **Step 4 Books** (grades 2–4) offer exciting nonfiction for the increasingly independent reader.

Text copyright © 2000 by Lori Haskins. Illustrations copyright © 2000 by Valeria Petrone. All rights reserved under International and Pan-American Copyright Conventions. Published in the United States by Random House, Inc., New York, and simultaneously in Canada by Random House of Canada Limited, Toronto.

www.randomhouse.com/kids

Library of Congress Cataloging-in-Publication Data
Haskins, Lori.
Ducks in muck / by Lori Haskins. p. cm. — (Early step into reading)
SUMMARY: Ducks escape from trucks that are stuck in the muck.
ISBN 0-679-89166-8 (trade). — ISBN 0-679-99166-2 (lib. bdg.) [1. Ducks—Fiction. 2. Trucks—Fiction. 3. Mud—Fiction. 4. Stories in rhyme.] I. Title. II. Series. III. Series: Early step into reading. PZ8.3.H2595Du 2000 [E]—dc21 98-45299

Printed in the United States of America February 2000 10 9 8 7 6 5 4 3 2 1

STEP INTO READING, RANDOM HOUSE, and the Random House colophon are registered trademarks and EARLY STEP INTO READING and colophon are trademarks of Random House, Inc.

Early Step into Reading™

Ducks in Muck

by Lori Haskins
illustrated by Valeria Petrone

Random House 🏠 New York

Ducks.

Trucks.

Ducks in trucks.

Trucks.

Muck.

Trucks in muck.

Trucks stuck.

Ducks stuck.

Stuck in muck.

What luck!

More trucks!

More trucks stuck.

Four trucks stuck.
Stuck in muck.

What luck!

More ducks!

Ducks unstuck.

Good-bye, trucks!

Good-bye, trucks
stuck in muck!

Ducks.

Trucks.

Yuck!